Monkey Tales II

SALLY JO MARTINE

COVER: Boqs (Pages 4 - 5); Photo: Alan Francescutti

ISBN-13: 978-0615821245
ISBN-10: 0615821243

DEDICATION

Dedicated to my mother, Helen Martin, whose playful and imaginative spirit lives on in each and every monkey.

AUTHOR'S NOTE

These handmade, one-of-a-kind original monkeys discovered themselves somewhere between the assemblage of their body parts and subsequent adornment.

Each monkey has their own story, yet they share a common purpose – to bring levity, light, and joy into the lives of others.

VISIT US ONLINE

OneBeingHuman-sjm.com

ACKNOWLEDGMENTS

I am so grateful to the growing base of monkey fans. You are now too numerous to mention, but you're part of the tribe, and you know who you are! Special thanks to Alan Francescutti, who deftly recorded each monkey with the photographic instincts of an animal, and Don Flora, who generously and patiently supplied expert design guidance. Alex arrived with a last-minute life boat, for which I'm extraordinarily thankful. Finally, many thanks to the Friends of the Library, Downtown Bremerton Branch. You are a force to be reckoned with, both individually and collectively.

All photographs are courtesy of Alan Francescutti.

ABRAM

Abram's first restless stirrings of inner conflict emerged as he was coming of age in the small Amish community of his birth. Esteemed by the elders as a virtuous boy, Abram had consistently demonstrated humility and obedience, and, according to tradition, it was time for his baptismal vows. Abram respected the values of his community, and he was grateful to have been adopted as an infant, but he had never given any thought to his roots. Now, on the brink of adulthood, it seemed important, and when he asked the elders, he was shocked to discover that his birth parents were the legendary Rafiya and Kelandra. No wonder he was overcome with such dizzying ethnic, cultural, and spiritual confusion! The fact that his hormones were raging only deepened his growing sense of conflict and displacement. On the one hand, he would finally be able to marry and have his own barn raising, but, for the first time, he saw an expanse of alternate scenarios, ways of being different in the world – perhaps he should pursue a tribal vision quest, join a drumming circle, or simply succumb to his Rastafarian nature and don the headphones, crank up the tunes, and light up.

BAM BAM

There would be plenty of time for worries to set in once he grew older, but for the time being, Bam Bam was happy to follow his sister Pebbles' lead, offering flowers to all, and sitting back to soak it all in. Undoubtedly the monkey that spurred Pebbles to action in the first place, Bam Bam's monkey-like appearance frequently incited specist slurs that Pebbles found appalling. Bam Bam came from a highly functional tribe, however, and his self-esteem remained intact, regardless of how he was treated. He could have let the whole thing slide, but Pebbles was persistent, he adored her, and he would do anything to support her endeavors, whether at the local or global level of action. Inevitably Bam Bam became the mascot for the whole movement. Strangely, no one found it ironic when marchers took up his name as the primary chant. The movement took place long before Americans turned their scrutiny towards the second amendment, and their rights to bear arms.

BOQS

A yeti monkey of tremendous stature and iridescent wonder, Boqs roams the mountainous forests in relative anonymity. Though many doubt his very existence, he inspires primal longings in those who believe. While sightings are legendary among the collectors of magic mushrooms, it remains unclear whether Boqs is geographically linked to the locations where psilocybin-containing mushrooms are commonly found or whether ingestion of the mushrooms themselves opens the mind in a way that facilitates a heightened state of "seeing." Regardless, there's a dearth of first-hand accounts, and those who have come forward report that a single gaze is akin to enlightenment. Boqs is purported to have supernatural capacities, and when he fastens his gaze on a mere mortal monkey, it penetrates with absolute illumination and transformative power, lighting every corner of the soul, and changing the "seeing" monkey forever.

CORY

Cory is an astonishingly rare unclassified catfish monkey from the Corydoradini tribe. His specialized anatomy is functionally tailored to address his unique physical and psychic needs. The frontal positioning of his eyes yields ocular mastery whether swimming or standing, his uniquely hinged legs afford him the speed of a cheetah – whether on land or at sea, and his helmet-like cranial encasement eases his feline-fashioned fears about underwater breathing. As a member of his species, Cory takes these attributes for granted, but as an actual catfish monkey, Cory suffers the self-conscious shame of being different from everyone he knows. As a monkey, he's specifically embarrassed by his lack of ears and tail. To make matters worse, he can't even hear what the other monkeys are saying about him! His crushing self-doubt regularly threatens to overtake him, but just when he feels his world is about to skid out of control, his feline nature comes to the rescue. He remembers that he is actually perfect...flawless even, exactly as he is.

7

ELOISE

Family, friends and neighbors knew early on that Eloise was destined to be a dancer. She twirled, swooped, dipped and kicked her way through nearly every activity during every waking hour. By the time she was a teenager, her entire identity hinged on the beauty she felt when dancing. With legs that "just didn't quit" and moves that revealed her pulsing awareness of every muscle and inch of her anatomy, she was a shoe-in for any audition. Her role as Bebe in the original Broadway production of *A Chorus Line* was key to the musical's instant success, and Eloise's spectacularly high kicks earned her feverish acclaim in the dancing world. Though she no longer performs, Eloise is still lithe, and the gracefully aging dancer is among the most sought-after dance instructors. She is widely believed to be the guiding genius behind Samba's stunning arrival on the international dance scene.

FRANK

Sinister at the core, Frank is an interdimensional being who freely wanders the portal between life and death. He uses his dark and villainous nature to wreak havoc everywhere he goes. He's highly influential and regularly employs his persuasive powers to spur others to ominous outcomes. Occasionally, Frank reminisces about the wild times he experienced during his 1960's upbringing and relaxes back into his primary nature as a free-spirited bunny monkey.

HELEN LOUISE

A smart cookie and a snappy dresser, Helen Louise held the firm view that looks mattered. She kept a trim figure alongside her good-looking husband whom she married (in her words) "because of his great teeth." Though he suffered gum disease in the early years of their marriage, he was a kind man with a good heart, and they looked good together for nearly six decades. After he was gone, Helen Louise continued to coordinate her attire, but she soon ascertained that there was more to life than being thin, and she began raiding the cookie jar on a regular basis. Her ever-slim shape gave way to that of a female fertility figure as commonly depicted throughout the ages.

HOOTY

Hooty has a need to know! The first-of-his-kind owl monkey is determined to learn everything there is to discover. Bookish and nocturnal, he has a penchant for spouting his wisdom ad nauseam, much to the discomfort of his compatriots. He carries on incessantly, long into each night, spewing fact after fact after fact. He's been approached multiple times by the SEA (Silence Enforcement Agency) but remains undeterred. Whenever he's taken in for questioning, he brings his interrogators up short, replying smugly, "Who?"

KELANDRA

Every time he dons his horny-nosed headdress, Kelandra is filled with the Great Spirit. The peaceful warrior wisdom of the rare and endangered rhino monkey slips over him, and he is immediately awash with the life force of all beings. Attuned to the pulsing presence of all that surrounds him – he hears the tiniest crickets in the far-off reed beds as well as the thundering hooves of the four-leggeds on the sunbaked plains. He is physically moved by the massive stone in the distant mountains, the beating wings of the ancient pterodactyls, and the slithering snakes in the skittering underbrush. The artificial barriers of time and distance recede the longer Kelandra dances, and he finds himself soon immersed in the round, beating heart-sphere of connection. Periodically, his mind drifts, and he remembers his powerful connection with Rafiya, the ethereal force of their union, the birth of their son, and the heart-wrenching decision to go their separate ways and leave Abram with the Amish.

KERMIT

Kermit is rarely anything but happy, and his lanky enthusiasm leaves him leaping from one adventure to the next. Though he has yet to form a committed romantic engagement like his grandfather Sven, Kermit is unabashed about sowing his wild oats and enjoys an immense appetite, of "frog-monkey" proportions. Despite his successful philandering, he is surprisingly clumsy, often referring to himself as having "two left feet." Consequently he's slightly envious of his Cousin Olaf's graceful athleticism, but Kermit has other gifts to savor. Most notably, he is musically gifted. In fact, he was recently adopted into a tribe of tango-loving performers who fervently condone his unrestricted activities across the musical spectrum, ranging from Latin, to classical, chamber, rock 'n roll, and even Tuvin throat singing.

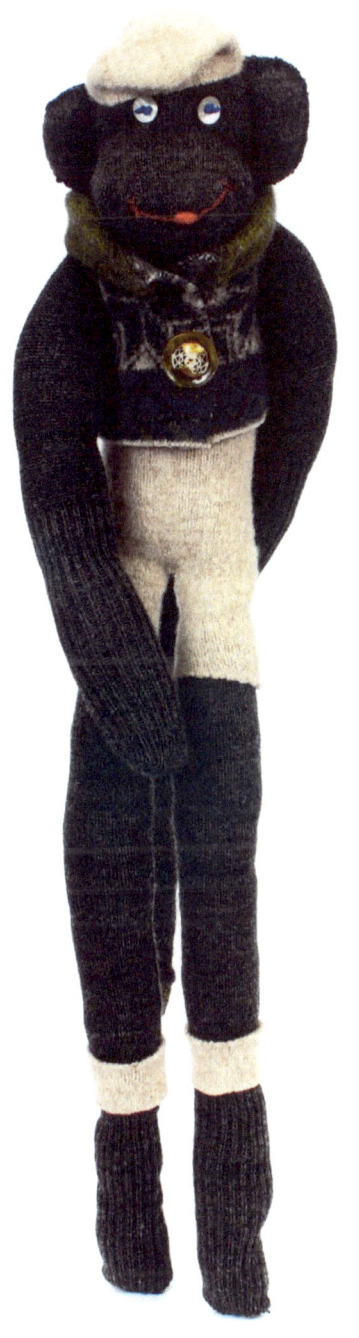

LULU

Lean and lanky Lulu, the long-legged Christmas elf monkey lives in a lovely loft in Lapland, Finland where she lends a hand at the local lost-toy outlet. Though often lonely and longing for a lyrical consort, she's learned that love will land in her heart when her spirit spills over. Her looks startle many, most of whom have never seen anyone so tall. But her luscious lips, matched only by the liquid, lustrous pools of her eyes will surely lure her lover's gaze in due time.

LUMEN

For Lumen, the world is a tapestry of color, weaving every hue along the spectrum and every point of saturation therein. Indoctrinated by a mystical and powerful peyote elder at an early age, Lumen is a long practitioner of the mythical "Luminec" arts. He is tuned to the inner vibrations of the universe and dances to the beat of his own entranced drumming. He brings his extra-sensory skills to every corner of his life – testing, tasting, and touching the nuanced fabric of being.

MARISOL

A statuesque Venezuelan monkey of inexorable beauty, Marisol is a sculptress by trade, and she's internationally esteemed for her creative genius and large scale radical works. Her most recent sculpture, however, stirred rumors among the art critics. "Orbit" was revealed at a spring fashion fundraiser for breast cancer survivors when Venus paraded up the runway wearing nothing aside from Marisol's celestial-styled headdress. Whereas Marisol's previous works notably addressed social justice issues that sparked community dialogue and controversy, this vaguely astral ornamental work seemed intensely personal. Critics speculated that it heralded a major shift in her artistic direction. Clearly a contemplative work, "Orbit" seemed to offer a glimpse into the artist's soul. Marisol read the reviews, and she knew the critics were on track. Her entire life was in upheaval. Her known world had shattered, and the broken pieces formed a frenzied orbital rotation around her very core. Yes, she had survived. But, bereft at the unfathomable departure of her monkey mate, she now asked herself, "How will I continue?" Marshaling the energy to participate in the recent breast-cancer fundraiser took immense reserves, but the cause was the only thing that seemed to ground her these days, and she is honoring that as her life continues to unfold, one day at a time.

MAXIMILLIAN

Like the "Jack in the Box" toy of his youth, Maximillian pops up at the most opportune and inopportune moments either wearing a huge smile or an expression that's vaguely sinister. Among the most generous and charming of cohorts, he frequently turns into a trickster – suddenly, and at seemingly random times. Over the years, his friends have been baffled, and they're often left wondering whether Maximillian is well-intentioned or not. He seems somehow duplicitous, rather like Jekyll & Hyde, though they would never venture to say such a thing to him directly. It's just that when he makes that shift so unexpectedly, he can seem a little bit maniacal. Startled by his mood swings, his friends often adopt an expression of fear, at which point the pattern inevitably repeats. Maximillian soon pops up with a hearty laugh and a big bear hug, reminding them that he's among their oldest and dearest of friends. How could they think such awful things about their childhood playmate?

PEBBLES

In her most fanciful daydreams, Pebbles has a flower for everyone. Like her idol Bob Marley, she just knows that "Everything's Gonna be Alright!" Pebbles was among the first monkeys to rally for her own "personhood." Revolutionary at its inception, the concept of inalienable rights for monkeys was rapidly assimilated into the global consciousness. Given her gentle persistence, unwavering advocacy, and generally positive demeanor, Pebbles was unequivocally the natural spokesmonkey, and it was these very attributes that kept the movement from turning sour. Simply holding her signature flower and raising it high above her head was a call to peaceful action among her followers.

PETER

Buoyant, often clairvoyant, and a renowned storyteller, Peter recently divined his "soul-nephew" relationship with Pablo. Revealed to him in a dream, the knowledge emerged as a burst of awareness, much the same as most things did with him. What Pablo painted on canvas, Peter shaped with words. This extraordinary gift was telepathically transported along the soul highway from the elder to the younger. Peter's childlike wonder and fanciful dreams paved the way for the transmission. Naturally inclined to set aside societal preconceptions and rigid constructs, Peter made a habit of tuning into his own inner child for guidance, and whenever he did, he gained direct access to the heartbeat of existence.

PHYLLIS

A renowned comedian and actress, Phyllis earned a devoted following for her commanding stage presence, eccentric attire, striking eyelashes, brash comments, and unconventional lifestyle. She found her way to the stage as a stand-up solo comedy act, and she wisecracked her way into the hearts of millions. A comedian monkey is an exceptionally rare breed, and Phyllis was hard-pressed to preserve her claim to fame when word surfaced about a certain anthropomorphist lawsuit against her. Sadly, she lost the battle, and faded into monkey obscurity. Today she lives a quiet life though frequently communes with her long-time friend and supporter, Eloise.

PIERRE

A dignified Frenchman with obscure ancestry, Pierre
the sock monkey was among the first-of-his-kind to be
discovered and rapidly brought the genetic
community to its knees. There he was drinking his
wine, eating his cheese, walking his dog on the "poo-
filled" streets of Paris – essentially minding his own
business (so to speak), when someone decided to
make a big deal about his heredity. (What was it with
people's need to test their genes these days, anyway?
It was something everyone seemed to be doing, but
he just couldn't care less!) Confident in his knit-wool
native heritage, he considered moving abroad and
changing his name to escape the incessant buzzing of
the Paparazzi since news of his genus rocked the
world. When not in the limelight, he takes a
philosophical approach to life and spends most days
pondering the universe and its deepest mysteries.

RAVEN

Raven's presence occupies a sacred space beyond time and physicality. A Thought Catcher of great power, legend has it that he's actually "Crow-Magnon" - an early modern monkey of the European Upper Paleolithic. His robust stance hints at an ancient wisdom spanning the ages. Folklore portrays him as the talisman of his many avid devotees who value his swift spirit, keen eyesight, and stealthy ways.

SOPHIE

A nurse by trade, Sophie is an exceptionally hard-working, competent, and nurturing sort who thrives when tending the needs of others. Intent on giving her patients the most skillful care available, she routinely works to expand her knowledge base, taking extra classes and attending seminars whenever her schedule allows. Her patients adore her, and just looking at her open-hearted expression makes it easy to see why. On the home front, Sophie's sophisticated ways take center stage each evening. A social butterfly, she loves planning parties, enjoys dancing, and prefers "dressing" for dinner. These habits may soon undergo some adjustment, as she recently learned she's pregnant. She'll be sad to shed those sleek evening gowns, but the news that she's pregnant more than makes up for it. She's thrilled to welcome a new life into her world!

SPARKY

A Papillion monkey of unbridled energy and athleticism, Sparky absolutely adores his mistress Veronica. He monitors her every move, hovers close, and rarely misses joining her in a cheer. Their synchronous tale dates back to when Veronica participated in a fundraiser for the local shelter. She was actually paid (!) to lead the cheers following each bid. Sparky was one of the many dog monkeys hoping for a new owner that day, and when he first saw Veronica cheer, it was love at first sight. Sparky's jumping skills were noteworthy, even for a Papillion, and he immediately began jumping, leaping upward in unison with each of Veronica's cheers. He quickly attracted Veronica's attention and captured her heart. They remain inseparable.

TRUDY LYNN

Trudy Lynn is a shy, sweet monkey with a wide open heart. Her compassionate nature is obvious to everyone she meets, and she's readily known for her spot-on insights into the true nature of others. Lately, she's turned her gaze on Herman. As the main clerk at the local library, Trudy Lynn witnesses Herman's weekly forays into the shelves, and the monkey she sees both troubles and endears her. On the one hand, she can't bear to see Herman despair over his unrequited affection for Sarah (a complete dead end given Sarah's unhealthy hyper obsession with Biker Dude). Still, Trudy Lynn intuits a real tenderness in Herman, and she knows he's looking for a mate. Amazingly, Herman doesn't even seem to know that he's "in the closet." But it's obvious to Trudy Lynn that Herman's attraction to Sarah is due to her fashion savvy…not her gender. Now that Herman's decided to room with Robert(a), maybe he'll break out of that closet and embrace himself fully. Trudy Lynn believes Robert(a) may be just the monkey to help Herman discover his true nature.

VENUS

Barring her impressive full-body ink work, Venus is as naked as the day she was born. Her tattoos give one the impression of coverage, but she dons clothing only when required. Venus is an emphatic nudist, a political activist, and flower child of the 60's. Apart from her glorious tats and vaguely astral headdress, she prefers to go through life unadorned. Shunning the consumer-oriented fever raging among her contemporaries, she's embraced the emerging philosophy of the downwardly mobile, and she fully adheres to a "less is more" policy. Believing that real value extends far above, below, and around anything to do with money, she strives to minimize her draining impact on the planet through such measures as thoughtful consumption, recycling, and cultivating a desire for enough rather than more. Her ideas and lifestyle have been met with derision by many over the years, but she's pleased to note the "small is beautiful" concept is taking hold in far reaching corners of the globe. Her "stripped down" trip down the runway at the spring fashion fundraiser for breast cancer placed her squarely in the spotlight. She hopes to take advantage of that: rousing sock monkeys everywhere to "stuff-shedding" action.

VERONICA

A former go-go dancer and cheerleader, Veronica just can't bring herself to shed her pom poms. Hyper enthusiastic about nearly everything she does, sees, and hears, she routinely breaks out into a cheer. This quality makes her both exciting and annoying to be around. She doesn't seem to have an "off" button, and her relentless "rah-rah's" can become tiresome, to say the least. Oblivious to these reactions, Veronica would be stunned to hear that her happy sounds were irritating. Her cup simply runneth over...incessantly. Fortunately for her, Veronica's need for a fan base is entirely fulfilled by Sparky, her constant companion and impeccable energy match.

THE MONKEY STORY

"Oh, Sally…" she said, on opening it. For her 89th birthday, I had been sorely challenged to find anything…anything at all to breathe life into her spirit and make her days less long. But my mother's very first sock monkey surprised us both. Tears of delight blanketed her face. She stretched out her arms, reached for it, and simply stared. Her mouth curled gleefully into a little-girl smile, and with eyes glistening, she cooed again, "Oh, ohhhhh, Sally…"

Amazingly, the monkey conveyed my mother straight to her youth, offering a direct portal into carefree days, where "hope" colored her entire horizon.

"Miss Princess Annabelle Liberty Shores," aka "Gertrude," became my mother's new best friend. Mom proudly carted her along everywhere, and promptly enlisted the nurses, aides, and residents in a naming contest. To my sister and me, the monkey was unmistakably "Gertrude." But Mom insisted on her lengthier, more formal name. "Gertrude" became my mother's constant companion, and I quickly saw "more monkeys" move to the top of my to-do list.

"Gertrude" launched a four-month journey of unforeseen happiness, adding companionship, anticipation, and joy to each new day. Dozens of monkeys followed, and Mom hosted countless "sleep-overs" for her rapidly expanding group of friends. The new spark in Mom's eyes was never about me. It was the life force behind the monkeys themselves that formed the real gift. This new cast of characters carved out their own stories, each sending a taproot into Mom's most fanciful dreams and memories.

Mom's sock monkey journey was inexpressibly rich…a treasure trove of simple pleasures feeding her entire family. As she moved out of this life and into whatever follows, she cradled her friend, and I can only imagine she drew comfort from not passing alone.

GERTRUDE

Gertrude's heavily-lashed eyes and wide red lips complement her somewhat misshapen limbs and strangely fashionable attire. The "original" monkey, she's undeniably ahead of her time and out of step with convention, but she's captivating in her ingenuity. Gertrude developed a special fascination for genealogy in her later years and recently discovered that she grew up a mere four miles from her contemporary, Agatha. Photo courtesy of Rex-zane Rudee.

ABOUT THE AUTHOR

Shaped by a free-range childhood in the Pacific Northwest, the author's work radiates from a deep and playful inner space.

As one among billions being human on the planet, she pairs language with design for clarity, beauty, and impact. Centering love as its compass, One Being Human gathers artistry, whimsy, and humility for each project.

Sally Jo's tiny 450sf home kindled her passion for minimalism and helped stretch her into the song she's here to sing. She's animated by peace, poetry, gardening, cooking, and sock monkeys.